I0640692

Henry William Dulcken

Golden Harp

hymns, rhymes, and songs for the young

Henry William Dulcken

Golden Harp
hymns, rhymes, and songs for the young

ISBN/EAN: 9783337266691

Printed in Europe, USA, Canada, Australia, Japan

Cover: Foto ©Andreas Hilbeck / pixelio.de

More available books at **www.hansebooks.com**

THE

GOLDEN HARP:

HYMNS, RHYMES,

AND

SONGS FOR THE YOUNG

ADAPTED

By H. W. DULCKEN, Ph.D.

WITH FIFTY-TWO ILLUSTRATIONS BY
J. D. WATSON, T. DALZIEL, AND J. WOLF.
ENGRAVED BY THE BROTHERS DALZIEL.

BOSTON :
ROBERTS BROTHERS.
1866.

TO

The Lady Mary Nisbet Hamilton

I DEDICATE THIS LITTLE BOOK;

GRATEFULLY MINDFUL

OF

THE KINDLY AND GENEROUS INTEREST

WHICH HAS ENCOURAGED ME

DURING ITS PREPARATION.

H. W. DULCKEN.

PREFACE.

THE Songs in this little Volume have been chosen from the works of thofe of the German Poets who wrote efpecially for the young. Matthias Claudius, for inftance, whofe rhymes for Children have found their way into every German collection of School Poetry, is the author of many of them. Rückert, who, turning afide from feverer ftudies, compofed many pieces to cheer the fick-bed of a little fuffering fifter, has not been forgotten : and fturdy Hans Sachs, the "Cobbler-Bard" of Nuremberg, has alfo been laid under contribution. In moft inftances I have tranflated the little poems as literally as the requirements of rhyme would allow ; here and there, however, fome verfes have been flightly altered, where a change in the form in which the ideas were conveyed feemed defirable.

In thofe of the Poems which have to do with facred fubjects, everything of fectarianifm has been carefully avoided. The broadeft principles of Chriftian truth alone are exhibited; with the object of infpiring love and gratitude, rather than of exciting terror—of awakening the fure and certain hope of glory rather than the fear of death and hell, in thofe little ones who, we are taught to believe, have received " not the fpirit of bondage again, to fear, but the fpirit of adoption, whereby we cry Abba, Father."

As regards Illuftrations, the figure fubjects are drawn by J. D. Watfon; the Landfcapes, by T. Dalziel; the Birds and Animals, by J. Wolf, and all moft carefully engraved by the Brothers Dalziel.

H. W. D.

CONTENTS.

c

X   *Contents.*

Contents.

xii   *Contents.*

THE GIVER OF GOOD.

CHILD, when with tending careful hand,
Amid the flowers you go,
Forget not Him, whose watchfulness
Sends rain on all below.

The same great Hand that guides the stars,
Pours down the fruitful shower ;
Then let the raindrops speak His love,
The stars proclaim His power.

13

CHARITY.—HELP WITH LOVE.

Inasmuch as ye have done it unto one of these, my brethren, ye have done it unto me."—Matthew xxvi. 40.

THINK, father, in thy curtained bed,
Thy dear ones round thee sleeping,
Of those who now keep hungry watch,
Whose life is toil and weeping.

Think of the widow's sleepless nights,
Her days of hard privation;
Her yearning for the vanished love,
Her care—her desolation.

Her orphan'd children—think of them ;—
Picture the dreary traces
Of pinching hunger, clouding o'er
Those little wistful faces.

Then think—oh think, who gave command,
These little ones to cherish,
Who said—*'Tis not your Father's will,
That one of them should perish.*

14

SEARCH THE SCRIPTURES.

SEARCH the Scriptures—words of truth—
Promises of gladness,
Teaching how to live and die,
Comforting in sadness.

Search the Scriptures—given for all—
Every clime and nation ;
They can make thee, simple child,
Wise unto salvation.

15

A SONG FOR THE NEW YEAR.

With welcome, and with cheerful song,
  We hail the new-born year,
Through joy and grief expected long,
  At length we see it here.

But many looked with hopeful eyes
  To greet this New Year's Day,
Who never lived to see it rise,
  For they were called away.

We will thank God, who let us live
  To see this year begun;
And pray that He his grace will give,
  Each day until 'tis done.

Be good, O Lord, to all—give Peace—
  Give each one what is best—
The poor man bread, the sick man ease,
  To all the weary, rest.

Be gracious, Lord, to all our band,
  And let us all, we pray,
Behold, within that better land,
  Thy brighter New Year's Day.

THE HEAVENLY FATHER.

"The Lord is good to all; and His tender mercies are over all His works."—Ps. cxlv. 9.

CAN you count the stars that brightly
Twinkle in the midnight sky?

The Heavenly Father.

Can you count the clouds so lightly
O'er the meadows floating by?
God the Lord doth mark their number
With his eyes, that never slumber;
    He hath made them, ev'ry one.

Can you count the insects playing
In the summer sun's bright beam?
Can you count the fishes straying
Darting through the silver stream?—
Unto each, by God in Heaven,
Life, and food, and strength are given;
    He doth watch them, ev'ry one.

Do you know how many children
Rise each morning, blithe and gay?
Can you count the little voices,
Singing sweetly, day by day?
God hears all the little voices,—
In their infant songs rejoices;
    He doth love them, ev'ry one.

THE LITTLE BIRD.

Among the trees at morning, there sang a little bird,
And loud through all the woodland his cheerful voice
was heard.

19

The Little Bird.

" O little bird, why sing you?" " Because I'm free
and gay,
I'm free and I am happy, this merry month of May."

There came a cunning fowler, slow creeping through
the glade,
And spread his hidden network beneath the greenwood
shade.

" O little bird why silent, that sang'st so loud of late,
Say, art thou so unhappy, within the wiry grate?"

" My joyful songs are ended,—I sang when I was free,
But lo, I am a captive,—no singing now for me."

" Who is this little birdie? And who the fowler, too?
You ask me, child, to tell you? My child I spoke of
you.

" While innocence and candour within your heart can
stay,
You're happy—oh ! so happy—like any bird in May.

" Sin is the cunning fowler—goes creeping through the
fields,
To catch you in his network—and woe to him that
yields.

The Two Houses.

" A thousand fetters hold him, from peace he soon must
   part,
And lose that chief of blessings, a grateful quiet heart.

" Then must he weep and suffer, like yon poor captive
   there—
So think of this, dear children, and oh, of SIN beware !"

THE TWO HOUSES.

THERE went a wise and a foolish man,
And each to build him a house began ;
One built on a rock, and one on the sand,
And when the two houses erect did stand,—
While the sun shone on them, no man could see
Which house of the two might the firmer be ;—
But when the dark sky began to frown,
And the wind, and the storm, and the rain came
   down,
The rock-built house bore the shock right well,
While its neighbour tottered, and crashing fell.
So those shall stand in the tempest's shock,
Who build on God's promise, the Bible rock,
While the hope that wars against God's command,
Shall fall with a crash, like the house on the sand.

THE BIBLE.

A TREE stood on a mountain,
And golden fruit it bore ;
Grew broad and tall, to be seen by all,
From shore to distant shore.

And men would come to seek it,
Nor ever came in vain ;
For the golden fruit around its root
Fell thick like autumn rain.

And yet the fruit decreased not
Upon its lofty crown,
As on the ground, and on all around,
The golden shower fell down.

For the fruit was given by God in Heaven,
In love and mercy free,   .
That, great and small, it might comfort all,—
And " the BIBLE " is that tree.

THE EVENING SUN.

GOLDEN sun of evening,
Beautiful to see ;
Not without emotion,
Can I look on thee !

Thou art now to leave us,
With thy beauteous ray,

The Evening Sun.

Over vale and mountain,
Wending far away.

From the steeple, chiming,
Sounds the belfry bell,
Like a voice of music,
Bidding thee farewell.

Many hands are folded,
And the voice of prayer
Mingles with their chiming
Through the evening air.

On the lofty steeple
Ling'ring light yet plays,
And the distant mountains
Gleam through purple haze.

Now the sun departing,
Leaves us in the night;
One still watcheth o'er us,
Who can give us light.

Thou, great God of wonders,
Dwell'st where all is pure;
Sun and moon shall vanish,
But Thou shalt endure.

24

The Holy Book.

Grant us, great Creator,
Thine own light to see,
That we turn our faces
Upward unto Thee.

THE HOLY BOOK.

In that Book so old and holy,
I would read, and read again,
How our Lord was once so lowly,
Yet without a spot or stain.

How the little children found Him,
How He loved them and caressed;
How He called them all around Him,
Took them to His loving breast.

How His pity, never-failing,
On the sick was sure to flow,
How the poor, the blind, the ailing,
Were His brethren here below.

How when each poor wand'rer sought Him,
Guilty, helpless, sorrowing sore,

The Holy Book.

He received, and helped, and taught him,
Bade him go, and sin no more.

With rejoicing hearts and grateful,
Let us read and still read on,

A Child's Hymn for Christmas.

How He was so true and faithful,
How He loved us, ev'ry one.

How, good shepherd, He did cherish
All the flock He came to save,
Watching, that not one might perish,
Of the lambs His Father gave.

Let us gladly kneel, and often,
Round His feet, that loved us best,
Then each stubborn heart He'll soften,
And in Him shall all be blessed.

A CHILD'S HYMN FOR CHRISTMAS.

Thou holy Jesus, kind and dear,
Who for us children camest here,
That, blest and purified by Thee,
God's little children we might be.

God sent Thee down, a light divine,
Through all this darkened world to shine,
A heavenly child, a heavenly ray,
To guide us all the heavenly way.

Joy Everywhere.

O holy Jesus, kind and dear,
Because thy birthday now is near,
For ev'ry child, in ev'ry clime,
It is a happy, joyful time.

Then bless me too, and from Thy throne,
Look down, Lord, on Thy little one,
Wash Thou my heart all pure and white,
In heavenly fountains clear and bright.

Lord, make me like the angels mild,
A loving, humble, grateful child;
That Thine I evermore may be,
Thou holy Jesus, grant to me !

JOY EVERYWHERE.

I HAVE been on the mountain
    That the song-birds love best,
They were sitting there, they were flitting there,
    They were building their nest.

I have been in the garden
    Where the busy bees did roam,
They were coming, all humming,
    To their straw-covered home.

28

Joy Everywhere.

I have been in the meadows,
The lambkins were there ;

On the mount, in the meadow,
There was joy ev'rywhere.

MORNING SONG IN SPRING.

How beauteous, how lovely, is ev'rything here!
The sun on the hill-side, the shade on the weir;
Where through the bright crystal the fishes are seen,
Where wave o'er the water the alder-trees green.

How glow the bright meadows with young verdure new!
How fresh bloom the flow'rets bespangled with dew!
The berry already is blushing in red;
The wheat-ear is smiling with promise of bread.

The slender birch waves in the whispering grove;
The bramble-bush twineth the rockstone above;
The honey-bee hums as he swiftly speeds on;
The frog's voice is drowned in the lark's sweeter tone.

How beauteous, how lovely do all things appear!
The waterfall's murmur, the shade on the weir.
On all sides around us pure joys are unfurl'd,
To light with their radiance our path through the world.

THE MOTHER'S SONG.

Sleep, my child, on mother's arm,
Safe from danger, safe from harm—
Teazing flies away shall flee,
Mother's love shall watch o'er thee.

God on high keeps watch and ward,
Child and mother He doth guard;
We His children, great and small,
Sleep in His protection all.

30

The Mother's Song.

Through the silent hours of night,
He can see thy slumbers light,

Hears each earnest prayer I've said,
Begging blessings on thy head.

THE IMMENSITY OF GOD.

Who can, on the seashore,
Count the grains of sand?
Or the leaves in Autumn,
Whirling o'er the land?

Or the winter snow-flakes
Driving fierce and free?

The Immensity of God.

Or the drops of water
In the briny sea?

Who can measure ocean,
Where it deepest flows?
Or the rays the sun darts
When it brightest glows?

Who, than swiftest lightning,
Faster yet can flee?
Name that wond'rous Being—
Greater none than He!

God is the unnumber'd,
Who no bound can know;
Suns and stars, before Him,
Are as flakes of snow.

God is called the Boundless,
Fathomless is He;
Swifter than the lightning,
Deeper than the sea.

WHAT THE MOTHER SAID TO HER CHILDREN ON A MAY MORNING.

THERE's something splendid here to see,
  Come, children, ope your eyes,
And call your father too, to me,
  The sun's about to rise.

How cheerfully it runs its course,
  And ne'er forgets its duty ;
Rises each morn renewed in force,
  Each evening sets in beauty.

Goes onward, shining day by day,
  O'er land and ocean ranging,
With milder or with fiercer ray,
  With ev'ry season changing.

Now this can not occur by chance,
  I scarce need stay to prove it;
The waggon yonder won't advance
  Till some one comes to move it.

And as the sun can't understand,
  Nor know what will betide it,
There must be ONE who with His hand,
  Like any lamb can guide it.

And that He's working but for good,
We know, whate'er betideth,

See how He strews His gifts abroad,
Although His hand He hideth.

What the Mother said on a May Morning.

He helps and blesses o'er and o'er,
    Gives food to all who need it;
Gives us the garden at the door,
    Our cow the grass to feed it.

'Tis He, dear children, gives you bread,
    Each pretty flower to please you,
And wheresoe'er your steps are led,
    Be certain that He sees you ;

Knows ev'rything you've thought and done,
    What caused you joy or weeping ;
He loves His children, ev'ry one,
    And all are in His keeping.

The beauteous stars that o'er us beam,
    The sun, so brightly shining,
The golden dawn, the silver stream,
    'Mid copse and forest twining ;

The violets blue, the flow'ring trees,
    That wave their boughs before us;
The " garment's hem," are, children, these,
    That He hath folded o'er us.

They're messengers, who mightily
    Can tell His mighty story—

36

What Man Can and What He Cannot Do.

The mirrors of His majesty,
The temple of His glory.

The world is one vast dwelling-place,
By master-hand erected,
Wherein His love and faithfulness
Are everywhere detected.

He dwells concealed, and all apart
From those who do not mind Him;
Yet seek Him, children, *with your heart*,
And surely ye shall find Him.

CLAUDIUS.

WHAT MAN CAN AND WHAT HE CANNOT DO.

A MAN may build, of polished stone,
A splendid house, with cunning hand;
But still he never can *create*
One single little grain of sand.
A man may crush the hardest stone,
Until in dust its fragments fly;
But all his strength will not suffice
E'er to destroy it utterly.
Whatever power he may employ,
He can't *create*, nor *aught destroy*.

37

THE BLIND MAN.

Dear children, see, I'm old and poor,
I grope my way from door to door.
You, happy children, cannot know
How dark the path through which I go.

53

But Bible words have comfort strong—
They're ringing round me all day long—
They tell me of a brighter place,
Where I shall see my Maker's face.

THE GREAT GIVER.

The Earth, in the beginning,
Was empty, void and drear ;
Nor, till the Lord had spoken
Could aught on earth appear.

'Twas thus, in the beginning,
When God the word did say ;
And as in the beginning,
It still is, ev'ry day.

He sets the sun his journey,
He holds the moon on high,
He guides the winds, and opens
The floodgates of the sky.

He gives us joy and gladness,
And makes us fresh and red,
He gives the ox his pasture,
And all their daily bread.

A Child's Evening Prayer.

And hearts to love and trust Him,
And spirits mild and meek;
And grace to bring me near Him,
All this from Him we seek.

For He can see in secret,
And ceaseless watch doth keep,
And those that pray in secret,
He touches, while they sleep.

O then, let praise and glory,
And thanks unceasing be,
To Him, the bounteous giver;—
There is none else but He.

A CHILD'S EVENING PRAYER.

Weary now I go to bed,
Close my eyes and rest my head;
Father, let Thy watchful eye
Be upon me, as I lie.

For the wrong I've done this day,
Look not on it, Lord, I pray;
But forgive the ill I've done,
For the sake of Christ, Thy Son.

A Child's Evening Prayer.

For my parents dear, I pray;
Father, take them not away;

Let us all in peace awake,
For Thy Son, our Saviour's sake.

HOPE FOR THE FUTURE.

When the wintry wind is blowing,
When the year's bright days have fled,
When the pretty flowers are faded,
And the gay green leaves lie dead,
With the Spring we say, still hoping,
Will return the flowers that fled.

To-Morrow.

When the son, from his father's dwelling,
Forth to foreign lands is led ;
When by the deserted fireside
Many bitter tears are shed,
"He'll come back," we say, " and with him
Will return the joy that's fled."

When on graves, where all in silence
Sleep the unforgotten dead,
Bright the quiet stars look downwards,
Then they smile as though they said,—
"They shall live again, and with them
All the joy that with them fled."

TO-MORROW.

" To-Morrow, to-morrow, but not to-day !"
That is what lazy people say ;
   " To-morrow I'll work, not now !
To-morrow that lesson hard I'll learn,
To-morrow from that sad fault I'll turn,
   To-morrow I'll do it, I vow."

And why not to-day, pray, let me ask?
To-morrow will have its appointed task,
   Each day will bring its own ;

43

The Beſt Guide.

I cannot tell what may happen anew,
I can only see what is next to do,
　　And a thing once done is done.

He who advances not, must retreat,
Our moments go onward beat by beat,
　　Not one of them comes again.
To act in the present I still have scope;
But as to the future for which I hope,
　　May not that hope be vain !

In the book of my life, each useless day,
That passes all unemployed away,
　　Is but an unwritten page.
Well then I'll keep striving on and on,
That some good deed on every one
　　May be written, from youth to age.

THE BEST GUIDE.

The father and his little son have been abroad to-day,
They're going home, but it is night, and they have lost
　　their way.

Now scans the boy each rock, each tree ; he's seeking
　　near and far,
Some landmark in the deep'ning gloom, to tell them
　　where they are.

The Beſt Guide.

But see, the father's steadfast gaze is fixed upon the sky,

He puts his trust in surer guides, the stars that gleam
on high.

The Music of Heaven.

The rocks and trees have nought to tell, they loom so
    dark and strange,
They point the way, the silent stars, that shine and
    never change.

Thus they came home—Ah, well for those to whom
    such faith is given,
Through all their journey here on earth, to seek their
    guide in Heaven.

THE MUSIC OF HEAVEN.

"What are the beauteous music sounds,
Dear mother, look and see,
That at the silent midnight hour
From slumber waken me?"

" I cannot hear them—cannot see—
Oh, rest in slumber mild,
There's no one singing to thee now,
My poor, my suff'ring child."

46

The Music of Heaven.

" It is not music here on earth
That makes my heart so light;

The angels call me with their song,
Oh, mother dear, good-night !"

THE STRANGE CHILD'S CHRISTMAS.

THERE went a stranger child,
As Christmas Eve closed in,
Through the streets of a town, whose windows shone
With the warmth and light within.

It stopped at every house,
The Christmas trees to see
On that festive night, when they shone so bright—
And it sighed right bitterly.

Then wept the child, and said,
"This night hath ev'ry one
A Christmas tree, that he glad may be,
And I alone have none.

" Ah! when I lived at home,
From brother's and sister's hand
I had my share, but there's none to care
For me in the stranger's land.

" Will no one let me in?
No presents I would crave—
But to see the light, and the tree all bright,
And the gifts that others have."

48

The Strange Child's Chriſtmas.

At shutter, and door, and gate
It knocks with timid hand,

But none will mark, where alone in the dark
That little child doth stand.

49

The Strange Child's Chriſtmas.

Each father brings home gifts,
Each mother, kind and mild ;
There is joy for all, but none will call
And welcome that lonely child.

" Mother and father are dead—
O Jesus, kind and dear—
I've no one now, there is none but Thou,
For I am forgotten here !"

The poor child rubs its hands,
All frozen and numb'd with cold,
And draws round its head, with shrinking dread,
Its garment worn and old.

But see—another child
Comes gliding through the street,
And its robe is white, in its hand a light,
It speaks, and its voice is sweet :—

" Once on this earth, a child
I lived, as thou livest yet—
Though all turn away from thee to-day,
Yet I will not forget.

" Each child, with equal love,
I hold beneath my care,

The Strange Child's Chriſtmas.

In the street's dull gloom, in the lighted room,
I am with them ev'rywhere.

" Here, in the darkness dim,
I'll show thee, child, thy tree—
Those that spread their light through the chambers
        bright
So lovely scarce can be."

And with its white hand points
The Christ-child to the sky—
And lo, afar, with each lamp a star
A tree gleamed there on high.

So far, and yet so near,
The lights shone overhead,
And all was well, for the child could tell
For whom that tree was spread.

It gazed—as in a dream—
And angels bent and smiled,
And with outstretched hand to that brighter land
They carried the stranger child.

And the little one went home,
With its Saviour Christ to stay,
All the hunger and cold, and the pain of old
Forgotten, and past away.

51

THE FOUR SEASONS.

SPRING.

Spring day—happy day!—
God hath made the earth so gay!
Ev'ry little flower He waketh,
Ev'ry herb to grow He maketh.
When the pretty lambs are springing,—
When the little birds are singing,—
Child, forget not God to praise,
Who hath sent such happy days.

SUMMER.

Summer day!—sultry day!
Hotly burns the noon-tide ray;
Gentle drops of summer showers
Fall on thirsty trees and flowers;
On the corn-field rain doth pour,
Rip'ning grain for winter store.
Child, to God thy thanks should be,
Who in summer thinks of thee.

AUTUMN.

Autumn day !—fruitful day !
See what God hath giv'n away !
Orchard trees with fruit are bending,
Harvest wains are homeward wending,
And the Lord all o'er the land
Opens wide His bounteous hand.
Children, gath'ring fruits that fall,
Think of God, who gives them all.

WINTER.

Winter day!—frosty day!
God a cloak on all doth lay;
On the earth the snow He sheddeth,
O'er the lamb a fleece He spreadeth,
Gives the bird a coat of feather,
To protect it from the weather,—
Gives the children home and food,
Let us praise Him—God is good

55

THE SONG OF THE SEED-CORN.

The sower sows with even hand,
The seed-corn o'er the softened land,
And wonderful, where it is sown,
The tiny seed-corn still lives on.

When safe within the earth 'tis laid,
A hidden power is soon displayed;
A little germ, so smooth and soft,
Soon rears its tiny head aloft.

Small, weak, and cold, it comes to view,
And begs for sunshine and for dew;
And then the sun from out the sky,
Looks down upon it pleasantly.

But now are coming frost and storm,
And flee for shelter man and worm;
The little seed can't run away,
But in the wintry field must stay.

And yet it does not come to harm,
Falls from the sky a mantle warm;

The Song of the Seed-corn.

And folded in its cloak of snow,
It sleeps through all the winds that blow.

When once stern winter's past and gone,
The lark sings loud and wakes the corn,

The Song of the Seed-corn.

For Spring brings flowers and blossom-sheen,
And decks the mead with freshest green.

And soon, with corn-ears slim and tall,
The pleasant fields are covered all ;
And like the green sea, to and fro
They wave with all the winds that blow.

Then hotly from the sky at noon,
The sultry summer's sun looks down,
Till all the blooming earth beneath
Lies crowned with beauteous harvest-wreath.

The reapers come, the sickle sounds,
The sheaves are piled, and upward mounts
The song of joy, at night and morn,
For Heaven's best gift to man—the Corn.

"God bless you !" when a child can say
    These words with all its heart,
That God to whom each child should pray,
    A blessing will impart.

SUNDAY.

God on high to man did speak :
Seven days are in the week-
Six of these to you I give ;
Ye must work that ye may live—
But the seventh day shall be,
Always set apart for Me,
That My servants may have rest,
And may learn of My behest,
That the voice of praise and prayer
May be lifted ev'rywhere.
Think, dear child, what God doth say
Of His holy Sabbath Day.

FOR THE EVENING.

O Lord, my father and my mother say,
That Thou dost hear when the children pray,
That there's none so small, of us children here,
But in Thy heart it is held most dear.
Father in Heaven, love also me,
And forget not Thy child's necessity.

A SONG OF PEACE.

PEACEFULLY wanders star on star,
　Up in the deep blue heaven,
Far from tumult and far from war,—
　Yonder, where rest is given.

Peacefully flows the silver brook,
　Here through the fresh green meadows;
And the bright stars like diamonds look,
　Mirrored amid its shadows.

A Song of Peace.

"Children, dear children, live in peace,"
  Soundeth from earth and heaven ;
For, until strife and quarrels cease,
  Never can peace be given.

Peacefully, then, should children dwell ;
  Each one should love his brother,
Always ready all strife to quell,
  And to forgive each other.

Then will our life, a stream of love,
  Glide like a quiet river,
Till we find, o'er the stars above,
  Peace that endures for ever.

WHERE'ER you see a little space,
There plant a little tree ;
A good deed should be done whene'er
There's opportunity.

GOOD COUNSEL.

A RHYME SIX HUNDRED YEARS OLD).

GUARD, my child, thy tongue,
That it speak no wrong ;
Let no evil word pass o'er it,
Set the watch of truth before it :
That it speak no wrong,
Guard, my child, thy tongue !

Guard, my child, thine eyes,
Prying is not wise ;
Let them look on what is right,
From all evil turn their light :
Prying is not wise,
Guard, my child, thine eyes !

Guard, my child, thine ear,
Wicked words will sear ;
Let no evil word come in,
That may cause the soul to sin :
Wicked words will sear,
Guard, my child, thine ear !

62

Two and One.

Ear, and eye, and tongue,
Guard while thou art young;
For, alas! these busy three,
Can unruly members be:
Guard, while thou art young,
Ear, and eye, and tongue.

TWO AND ONE.

Two ears and only *one mouth* have you,
  The reason, I think, is clear,
It teaches, my child, that it will not do
  To *talk* about all you *hear*.

Two eyes and only *one mouth* have you,
  The reason of this must be;
That you should learn that it will not do
  To *talk* about all you *see*.

Two hands and only *one mouth* have you,
  And it is worth while repeating;
The *two* are for work you will have to do,
  The *one* is enough for eating.

PLOUGHMAN.

Child, hast thou seen the ploughman?
Look not on him with scorn,
For that his face is homely
And his raiment old and worn.

The Approach of Autumn.

Remember God hath called him
Unto a lowly state,
And taught him how to plough the land,
And sow the seed—and wait;

Till He Himself in kindness
Looks down upon the field,
And makes it, in His own good time,
A plenteous harvest yield.

Because God loves the ploughman,
A blessing sendeth He;
And grants him bread that he may eat,
And also, child, for thee.

THE APPROACH OF AUTUMN.

Now the woods are mellow;
Stubble fields are yellow;
  Autumn tints the trees;
Ruddy leaves fall daily;
Mists are rising greyly;
  Colder blows the breeze.

K

TIMELY ADVICE.

When once the arrow is shot away,
No earthly power can bid it stay;
When once the torrent foams deep and wide,
The cottage is whelmed in the foaming tide.
'Tis thus with the words that children speak,
Like flood or like arrows forth they break;
Shut the gate of thy lips, child, if thou'rt wise,
When *anger* begins in thy heart to rise.

GOOD SERVANTS.

My servants are a worthy crew,
The names of the men are " Work-to-do,"
And " Up-betimes," and " Earn-my-wage ; "
While the maids are called " Orderly," " Thrifty," and
    " Sage."

My butler and cook are " Hunger " and " Thirst,"
But of all my helpers, the foremost and first,
Are two, whose names are " Good Conscience," and
    '" Prayer,"
And I sleep in quiet while they are there.

LIVE IN PEACE.

Look at the doves on the roof-tree there,
Brother and sister, always a pair ;
In sunshine bright, and in rainy weather,
They love each other and keep together.

Little children, in child-like love,
You should be like the gentle dove,
Ever ready in peace to live,
Slow to offend, and quick to forgive.

PATIENCE.

On silent wings, an angel
Through all the land is borne,
Sent by the Gracious Father
To comfort them that mourn.
There's blessing in his glances,
Peace dwells where'er he came,
Oh! follow when he calls thee,
For *Patience* is his name.

Through earthly care and sorrow
He'll smooth the thorny way,
And speak with hopeful courage,
Of brighter, happier day ;
And when thy weakness falters,
His strength is firm and fast,
He'll help to bear thy burden,
He'll lead thee home at last.

Thy tears he never chideth,
When comfort he'd impart,
Rebuking not, he quiets
The longings of thy heart.

Perſevere.

And when, in stormy sorrow,
Thou murmuring askest " Why? "
He, silent yet, but smiling,
Points upward to the sky.

He will not always answer
Each question that's addrest,
His maxim is " Endure thou,
And after toil comes rest."
Through life, if thou wilt love him,
Thus by thy side he'll wend,
Oft silent, ever hopeful,
Still looking to the end.

PERSEVERE.

The fisher who draws in his net too soon,
  Won't have any fish to sell ;
The child who shuts up its book too soon.
  Won't learn any lessons well.

For if you would have your learning stay,
  Be patient, don't learn too fast ;
The man who travels a mile each day,
  Will get round the world at last.

UNDER THE GREEN TREES.

SUPPOSE the earth were barren and bare
Where the pleasant trees now stand,
On my word it would not be half so fair,
Nor half such a happy land.

70

Under the Green Trees.

If there were not around us a single tree,
  O'er our heads not a branch or spray,
The place would be gloomy and bare to see,
  And then we might run away.

But now we are happy as fish in the sea,
  Right gladly here we'll stay,
Then hail to every giant tree,
  To every tiny spray.
No man hath ever known or said
  How many there may be;
But each tree helpeth to make a shade,
  Each leaf to make a tree.

On the sofa sitteth the baron bold
  Whose servants on him wait,
The monarch sits on his throne of gold,
  And we sit here in state
On the fresh green grass 'neath the spreading tree,
  At ease in the greenwood shade,
Nor forget we to thank Him gratefully
  Who for us this place hath made.

CHILD'S EVENING PRAYER.

Now with weariness opprest,
I would close my eyes and rest,
Let Thine eyes, Our Father, be
On the child that prays to Thee.

For the wrong that I have done,
Look not, gracious Lord, thereon,.
Thy great mercy makes it good,
Through our dear Redeemer's blood.

Those that love me, great and small,
Lord protect them, one and all ;
Let all men Thy mercy share,
Ev'ry creature, ev'rywhere.

Eyes that watch, close Thou again,
Sooth the heart that beats in pain ;
Send, O Lord, Thy angel bright,
To be with us through this night.

SOLOMON AND THE SOWER.

In the field the wise king Solomon,
Had under Heaven set up his throne;
Then sees he near him a sower stride,
Who scattered seed on ev'ry side.

Then said the king, " What dost thou there?
Yon barren ground yields harvest ne'er;
Cease now thy toil and labour vain—
The seed thou'st sown thou wilt not gain."

The sower now, with checkèd hand,
In deep reflection still doth stand;
His arm then lifting sturdily—
To the wise king he made reply :—

" I've nothing else, beyond this field,
I've ploughed the land that it may yield;
I take no thought, no wealth possessing,
I give the corn, God gives the blessing."

MORNING SONG IN THE COUNTRY.

Come out of your beds, there,
    The cock loudly crows—
The birds they are singing,
    The morning wind blows;
And see, the red morning
    So gaily is here,

74

Morning Song in the Country.

On meadow, on brooklet
  The sunbeams shine clear.

Take coats from the cupboard,
  Take hats from the wall,
Take scythe, and take sickle,
  And hayfork, and all ;
The maids to the meadow,
  The men to the field,
That corn-field and hay-field
  Good harvest may yield.

And while ye are sowing
  And ploughing for food,
Look gratefully up to
  The Giver of good,
Who sends us our bread,
  By His mercy and power,
And blessing, and increase,
  And sunshine, and shower.

————

When the cock crows loud on the roof-tree tall,
  The moon snuffs out her light ;
Then out of your beds, little sleepers all,
  It's time to be brisk and bright.

75

WINTER.

Old winter is a sturdy one,
    And lasting stuff he's made of,
His flesh is firm as iron-stone,
    There's nothing he's afraid of.

Winter.

He spreads his coat upon the heath,
　　Nor yet to warm it lingers,
He scouts the thought of aching teeth,
　　Or chilblains on his fingers.

Of flowers that bloom or birds that sing,
　　Full little cares or knows he,
He hates the fire and hates the Spring,
　　And all that's warm and cozy.

But when the foxes bark aloud,
　　On frozen lake and river;
When round the fire the people crowd
　　And rub their hands, and shiver—

When frost is splitting stone and wall,
　　And trees come crashing after,
That hates he not, he loves it all,
　　Then bursts he out in laughter.

His home is by the North Pole's strand
　　Where earth and sea are frozen,
His summer-house, we understand,
　　In Switzerland he's chosen.

The Green City.

Now from the North he's hither hied,
　To show his strength and power,
And when he comes, we stand aside,
　And look at him, and cower.

THE GREEN CITY.

Children, I know of a wondrous town,
Where the houses are green the whole street down;
Some of them great, and some of them small,
Who likes may enter, they're open all.

I cannot aver that the streets are straight,
For they wind about at a comical rate;
But after all, would it pleasant be,
To be going straight on continually?

All the paths, and the roadways too,
Are spangled with flowers of various hue;
Smooth and soft is the pavement found,
And in colour 'tis like the houses around.

Many the people therein that dwell,
And all of them love their town right well;
This love for their home herein is seen
That each will sing, in his house so green.

78

The Green City.

The people are certainly somewhat small,
They are but little birds, one and all,

And, in short, this town so fair and good,
Is commonly called the gay Green Wood.
79

CUCKOO, NIGHTINGALE, AND ASS.

One day, within a pleasant vale,
The Cuckoo and the Nightingale
   Resolved to stake a dinner;
Each one in turn should sing his lays,
And he who gained the greatest praise,
   Should be declared the winner.

The Cuckoo said, " Ere we begin,—
I've found a judge—we'll call him in,—
   I mean the Ass, good brother;
His ears, you see, are large and long,
He'll hear each note of all our song,
   Where find we such another? "

Away to Master Ass they flew,
Who said he'd give a judgment true,
   Just as his friends had planned it.
The Nightingale first strained her throat,
Says Neddy, " I don't like your note,
   I can't quite understand it."

The Cuckoo then began to cry,
In tuneless accents, harsh and high;
   Then said the judge sedately :

The Mastiff and the Cat.

"I think no singer can be found,
So fine, in all the country round,
And he hath pleased me greatly."

THE MASTIFF AND THE CAT.

An honest old mastiff was lamed by a blow,
Defending his master, by robbers laid low;
With nothing to eat, and no place to lie down,
He mournfully limped through the streets of a town,
Where by chance he encounter'd, not far from the gate.
A cat who had met with a similar fate;
His leg had been crushed by the Abbot's fierce cook,
Because from the larder a partridge he took.

'Tis said that misfortune soon makes people known,—
They talked of their troubles, each mourning his own;
Till at last, quoth grimalkin,—"We'll go through the
        land,
Like faithful companions, and beg, hand in hand."

"No, no!" cried the mastiff, "that never would do,
We're both of us lamed in like manner, 'tis true,
But still, I don't wish to be taken for you."

THE POPLAR AND THE PLUM-TREE;

OR,

SHOW AND USE.

The Poplar said—said he,
To the little meek Plum-tree—
   " *For the little blue plum*
   That on you can come,
Why should you show such glee ? "

" *Yes, very glad am I,*"
The Plum-tree he made reply,
   " *That I furnish food,*
   And am not mere wood,—
A stick that grows up high."

Then the Poplar turned quite red ;
" *I may be a stick,*" he said ;
   " *But don't you see,*
   You poor little Plum-tree,
How high I can carry my head ? "

——— · ———

When *Work* comes into a house to stay,
Then *Want* will speedily flee away ;
But let Master *Work* once go to sleep,
And *Want* will in at the window peep.

82

WORK FOR ALL.

No twig on the green wood stands idle and still,
    Not a bee but some honey he'll win;
The stream bears the boat, or turns the mill,
    And the breeze blows out and in.
Then, away to your tasks, dear children, hie!
    To school with you, ev'ry one!
And happy is he whom Industry
    Will help till his work is done.

THE TWO DOGS.

A LITTLE lord two dogs did own,
They were a poodle and his son,—
Young Pantaloon, the puppy gay,
His lord's spare time would while away.
For he could dance, or stand on guard,
Or drag the go-cart round the yard;
Could through the deepest water swim,
Or beg, to please his master's whim.

Young Fred, the keeper's clever son,
Had taught the dog these tricks, this fun—
Who quicker learned, by line and rule,
Than many children learn at school.
It struck the little lord one day,
That there must be an easier way
To teach the big dog all this fun,
Than to instruct the little one.

The guardian of the house, poor Gruff,
Was a good honest beast enough,
But no one yet to school had brought him,
Or any learned tricks had taught him.
My lord to train him, once for all,
Propped up poor Gruff against the wall,
But all his efforts were in vain,
The dog each time fell down again.

The Stars at Night.

And now Professor Fred came too,
And tried the utmost he could do,
But though his best each tried in turn,
The hoary scholar would not learn.

"Perhaps," said Fred, "the stick will do,"
So Gruff was cuffed and beaten too,
But still was stupid as an owl,
And finally began to growl—
"What do you want?" the poor dog said.
"You'll never get my old grey head
To understand one thing you teach;
But hear the moral I can preach—
Good children, learn e'er youth is o'er,
When once you're old, you'll learn no more."

THE STARS AT NIGHT.

When you're all in bed at home,
  Then wakes up each star,
And the white wing'd angels come
  Floating from afar;
All night long their watch they keep
By the beds where children sleep.

85

THE REWARD OF GOOD NATURE.

The boy stood under the apple tree
    But could not reach the bough,
And longed for a prize from the store he could see,
    That hung in the leafy house.

The Reward of Good Nature.

And lo! the old tree its leafy crown
In the breeze shook to and fro,
Till a shower of apples came raining down
On the startled boy below.

He ate as long as eat he could,
But could not eat all that fell,
But receiving so much in wanton mood,
He wished for more as well.

An apple into the donor's face
He hurled, as if in joke,
And laughed to see how from its place
A comrade ripe it broke.

And all that fell around the root
He flung up, and thus maintained
The game, until of the luscious fruit
Not one on the tree remained.

Now what may the plundered tree have thought,
When there were no more to fall?
" I gave thee too much, I denied thee naught,
And thou hast robbed me of all."

THE DANCING BEAR.

Come boys, come, here's the bear—the bear,
With tramping tread he is dancing there,—
The man with wallet, and rope, and staff,
Will make him dance, and he'll make us laugh ;
While the rub-a-dub drum, and the too-too fife,
Make music that suits him just to the life.

A slothful brute is the lazy bear,
Sleeps half his life in his frowzy lair,
And thus, as we all may well suppose,
He gets from his keeper good store of blows ;—
Now if from punishment you'd be free,
Don't you be as idle and dull as he.

A greedy mouth has the dainty bear,
Where bees can be robbed, you'll find him there,
The bees in revenge make a gallant fight,
And sting him bravely,—and serve him right ;—
And I think from this we may soon discern,
What a bad reward greedy pilferers earn.

A sulky brute is the grumbling bear,
With his great gruff voice that sounds ev'rywhere ;

The Quail and her Young.

Dear children, when for a fault you're chid,
Mind you don't growl as the big bear did;
Lest you should be served like him, who goes
With an iron ring through his sulky nose.

The bear, the bear, the great gruff bear,
The lazy, the greedy, the grumbling bear,
Let him be off—let him go his way,
We've seen quite enough of him to-day ;—
We'll work, be contented, and speak folks fair,
Lest we should be like the great big bear.

THE QUAIL AND HER YOUNG.

WHERE the golden wheat-field was waving tall,
The quail built a nest for her young ones all.
One morn at daylight abroad she flew,
And homeward came with the evening dew ;
Then cried the nestlings, quaking with fear,
" O mother! a terrible danger is near,
The lord of this corn-field, the terrible man,
Came by here to-day with his son, and began,
' The wheat-ears are ripe, the harvest we'll keep,
Go, call thou our neighbours to-morrow, to reap.' "

The Quail and her Young.

" Indeed," said the Quail, " then no haste need be made,
Not willing are neighbours to render their aid."
And again at morning abroad she flew,
And came not home till the evening dew ;
Then cried the nestlings, quaking with fear,
" O mother ! another sad danger is near :
The lord of the corn-field, the terrible man,
Came by here again with his son, and began,—
' Our neighbours are faithless, and came not to-day—
Go to our relations to-morrow, and say :
We count on your kindness, to you we've appealed,
For aid to my father in reaping his field.' "

" Oh, then," said the Quail, " no haste need be made,
Relations are tardy to render their aid."
And again at morning abroad she flew,
And came not home till the evening dew ;
Then cried the nestlings, quaking with fear,
" O mother ! the greatest of dangers is near,
The lord of this corn-field, the terrible man,
Passed by here again with his son, and began,—
' Our faithless relations have failed us, I see,
I'll reckon alone on myself and on thee ;
To-morrow, ere cockcrow, we'll rise from our sleep,
And turn out together, the corn-field to reap.' "

The Quail and her Young.

" Indeed," said the Quail, " our time's drawing near—
Prepare then, my children, we must not stay here ;
Who by cousins and neighbours his work would have
    done,

Will find the day gone ere the task is begun :
It is by the efforts himself can bestow
His work will be finished, will prosper and grow."

The Quail, with her brood, fled away then and there—
And ere the next evening the corn-field was bare.

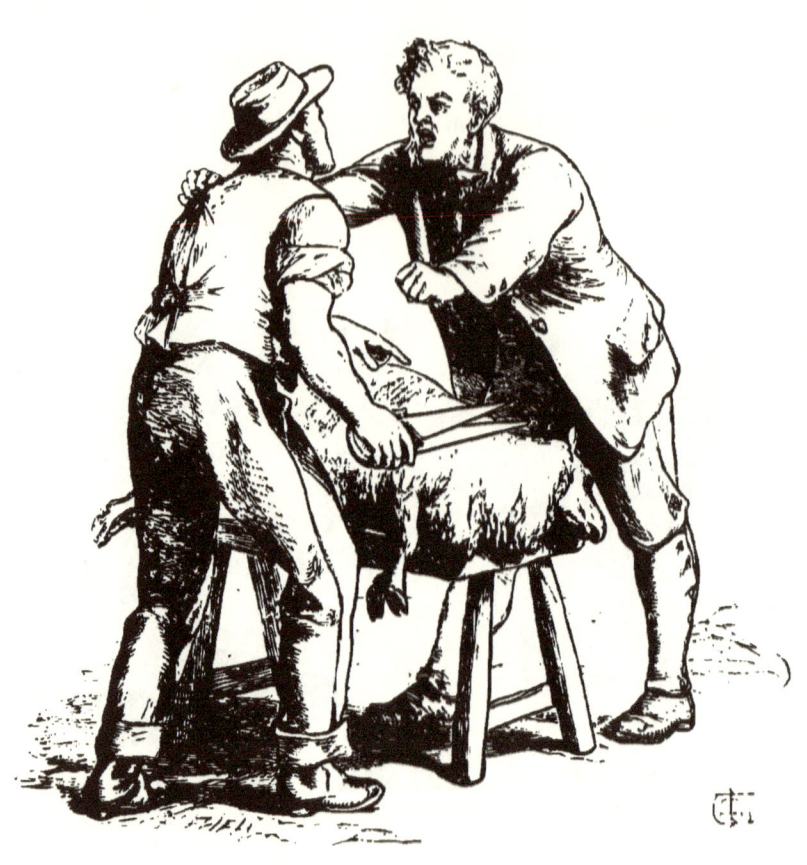

MALEY AND MALONE;

OR,

THE EVILS OF QUARRELLING.

Upon a sea-girt island, there dwelt two shepherds sly ;
The one was named Maloné, the other was called
Maley.

92

Maley and Malone.

A flock of sheep had been left them, that both of them
    should keep ;
Maley and Maloné were ruined, and all through the
    flock of sheep.

They pastured at first together, but ever at war they
    were ;
If one said, " Here we will pasture," the other would
    say, " No—there."
At last they said, " We'll divide them ;" but there
    was one odd sheep,—
And for this one they quarrelled, and lost their rest
    and their sleep.

Maloné said, " We'll kill it, and halve it by-and-by."
" First we must have its wool, though," objected at
    once Maley.
Maley he wanted stockings :—" Come, shear we it to-
    night."
" It's not the time," said Maloné, and so he refused
    outright.

" I'll shear my side of the sheep, then,—shear your's
    when you will ;"
Maloné would not have it, but Maley did it still.

The Blackbird.

The sheep was caught by a whirlwind, down a mountain gorge it rolled;
They got it out in the morning, but it was dead and cold.

" Maley, that sheep has been frozen through being shorn by you ! "
" No, no ; 'twas the wind that caught it, through your not shearing it too.
If you'd only done as I did, it had not thus been caught ;
For it would have kept its balance, had you shorn it as you ought."

Each went before the judges, complaining with rueful face,
" Aha ! " said the worthy lawyers, " what an interesting case ! "
And so the books were opened, and so the strife went on;
And when the shepherds were ruined, the cause was lost and won.

THE BLACKBIRD.

A MERRY blackbird, dark as coal,
With yellow bill like gold,
Dwelt where out-flowing from the rock
A silver streamlet rolled ;

94

The Blackbird.

And happily her jocund song
Through all the woods she trolled.

And see, amid the gay green leaves,
With beauteous crimson flush,
A bunch of berries glittered red
From out the shady bush,
And like a dart the foolish bird
On the tempting bait did rush.

But hidden 'mid those berries bright,
There lurked a cruel snare,
To hold the careless bird, prepared
Of strongly twisted hair;
And scarce a berry had he seized,
Ere it caught him unaware.

Dear children, from this story take
A warning, good and true,
Whene'er forbidden pleasures lure
The snare is lurking too,
So let temptation's berries hang
Untasted still by you.

THE IDLE BOY.

I DON'T like horses that will not spring,
And I don't like bells that will not ring;
I don't like firewood that will not burn;
I don't like mill-sails that will not turn,
And lazy children who will not learn.

CHILD'S PLAY.

The boy who's never tired of play,
Who seeks life's joy in sport alway,
That boy, I'm certain, never can
With growing years become a man.

The girl whose sole and only joys
Are centred in her dolls and toys,
That foolish girl herself will be
A doll, some day, assuredly.

For those alone who keep in view,
The wish *to learn* their whole life through,
The certain happiness can find,
To grow in sense, and heart and mind.

———

Not a creature so lowly in state,
  But God will look down on its pain ;
For nothing that God did create,
  Was ever created in vain.
Not a hair can fall off from our head,
  Not a bird from the roof, without Thee,
Then deign Thou, in grief and in dread,
  O Lord, our protector to be.

SIN AND PUNISHMENT.

Through all the land, on mischief bent,
   (And woe to him to whom they came),
A band of evil beings went,
   And Sin, or Crime was each one's name.

The grass was withered where they passed,
   The woods and meadows still as death,
And Nature seemed to stand aghast,
   And shudder at their poisonous breath.

By chance they turned,—then saw they one,
   An aged man, all bowed and bent,
Who with a crutch came creeping on,—
   They knew his name was Punishment.

" Ha ! ha !" they cried, " we will not wait !"
   But Punishment replied, secure :
" I'll overtake you, soon or late,
   I may be slow, but I am sure."

OX, ASS, AND LION.

Ox and Ass were once disputing,
As they wandered through the field,
Which of them might be the wiser;
Neither conquered, none would yield.

True Friendſhip.

And at last they both consented
That the Lion, speedily,
Should decide the weighty question ;—
Who could better judge than he?

So, with most respectful bearing,
Came they to the Lion's throne ;
He, with scorn that he concealed not,
On the kneeling pair looked down.

When they craved to hear his verdict,
This his Majesty did say :—
" Both of you are fools undoubted ;"—
So they stared—and went their way.

TRUE FRIENDSHIP.

THE friend who shows me myself in a glass,
Nor lets e'en the smallest failing pass,
Who will kindly warn, and can chide me too,
When I've left undone what I ought to do ;
  My friend is he,
  Though he seem not to be.

But he who can never censure me,
Whose words are the words of flattery,

The Recognition.

Who succour and aid to my faults hath lent,
Who waits not to pardon till I repent;
    My enemy is he,
    Though he seem not to be.

THE RECOGNITION.

A WEARY wanderer, staff in hand,
Comes home at length, from a foreign land,
Disfigured with dust, and with many a stain,—
Now who will be first to know him again?

So he enters the town, through the dear old gate,
And just by the barrier the toll-man sat—
The toll-man had been his comrade tried,
And oft in time past had sat by his side;
But see, the good toll-man no likeness can trace
To his comrade of old, in the sunburnt face.

And still through the streets he wanders on,
And a tear on his sunburnt cheek falls down—
See, his sister looks down from a lattice high,
And he greeteth her kindly, passing by;
Not even his sister the features can trace
Of the brother she loved, in the sunburnt face.

The Recognition.

And still through the streets he wanders on,
And the tears come thick—and he's still unknown.

There creeps from the churchyard his mother so gray,
"God greet you!"—is all that the youth can say—

Good Wine.

But see, she sinks, with a sob of joy—
" My son ! my son !" on the neck of her boy.

Though his face was tanned, though years had gone
    by,
No change could deceive the mother's eye.

GOOD WINE.

The best of wine for children, it is the pure white wine
That gushes from the mountain whereon the sunbeams
    shine ;
It flows through wood and meadow, where bird and
    insect play ;
It gives no child the headache, drink deeply as he
    may ;
And if it's best for children, as all good people tell,
Methinks it must be wholesome for grown-up folks
    as well ;
For many have been rescued from illness and from
    pain,
The day they took to drinking the pure white wine
    again.

THE LITTLE BOY WHO WANTED TO BE TAKEN EVERYWHERE.

JUST think ! the little boy went one day,
Into the meadows green, to play,
Then he was tired, rather,
And said, " I can't go farther—
I only wish that any one
Would come this way, and take me on."

Then came the streamlet gurgling down,
And offered to take the little boy on ;
So on a little log sat he,
And gaily cried, " This pleases me !"

But only think ! so cold was the river,
The little boy began to shiver ;
He grew chilly, rather,
And said, " I'll go thus no farther—
I only wish that any one
Would come this way, and take me on."

Then came the little boat floating down,
And offered to take the little boy on—
Then in the little boat sat he,
And gaily cried, " This pleases me !"

But you must know, the boat wasn't wide,
And the boy might soon fall over the side ;

The Restless Little Boy.

Then he was frightened, rather,
And said, " I'll go thus no farther—
I only wish that any one
Would come this way, and take me on."

Then came a big snail crawling down,
And offered to take the little boy on—
So on the snail-shell down sat he,
And gaily cried, " This pleases me !"

But what do you think—the snail lagged so,
For the little boy it was far too slow ;
He grew impatient, rather,
And cried, " I'll go thus no farther—
I only wish that any one
Would come this way, and take me on."

Then came a horseman riding down,
And offered to take the little boy on ;
So at the horseman's back sat he,
And gaily cried, " This pleases me !"

But fancy ! they went on like the wind,
Too fast for the boy who rode behind ;
He was jerked and jolted, rather,
And cried, " I'll go thus no farther—
I only wish that any one
Would come this way, and take me on."

The Restless Little Boy.

The branch of a tree caught in his hair,
And hooked the little boy then and there ;

And so he hung at the end of a bough,
And unless he's got loose he hangs there now.

THE RIDDLES OF THE ELVES.

The elves they sat in the rocky shaft,
And chatted away, all night, and laughed;

They asked these riddles, one by one,
Which, if not gold, had a golden tone,—

And when the morning breezes blew,
Away flew the elves, or melted like dew.

" What gold in no mine may ever lie ?"
" The gold of the sun that comes from on high."

" Who borrows his silver from foreign gold ?"
" The silver moon that hath o'er us rolled."

" What tear wells up from the hardest breast ?"
" The spring that hath lain in the rock at rest."

" What's the widest bridge that can span a lake ?"
" The ice-bridge—built of a single cake."

" What flood may ne'er from its home depart ?"
" The stream that flows through the human heart."

The Riddles of the Elves.

"Who is it mourns in his gayest gown?"
"The tree, when in autumn its leaves fall down."

"Who sees not the inside of his own home?
"The snail, though he never departs therefrom."

"Where have they made the smallest the king?"
"The kingfisher is but a weak small thing."

"When does the weak tread down the strong
Man crushes the earth as he walks along."

"What is stronger than firm-set ground?"
"The plough that tears it with many a wound."

"What is stronger than iron or brass?"
"The fiery flame that melteth the mass."

"What is stronger than fiercest fire?
"The watery stream that can queuch its ire."

"What more strong than the waves that flow?
"The wind that driveth them to and fro."

"What is stronger than wind and air?"
"The thunder,—they tremble when that is there."

" Why does not water flow uphill?"
" Because to flow downward is easier still."

" Why are the fishes dumb alway?"
" Because they've no clever things to say."

" Who can answer these riddles true?"
" Whoever knoweth a rhyme thereto."

" And wherefore do I now give o'er?"
" Because I wish to hear no more."

THE WHITE HART.

THREE hunters went to the wood one day,
The merry white hart to kill and slay.
They went to sleep in the sun's bright beam;
They woke, and then each man told his dream.

THE FIRST HUNTER SAID :—
" I dreamt I went and bent on the bush,
And the hart came bounding out, pish, push ! "

THE SECOND SAID :—
" I dreamt, in front of the hounds he sprang,
And then that I fired at him, bing, bang ! "

The White Hart.

" I dreamt that the stag on the ground I saw,
And merrily blew my horn, tra-ra ! "

As thus the three hunters talking lay,
The white hart himself ran by that way ;
And before the hunters had marked him well,
He was up and away through dingle and dell,
    Pish push, piff paff, tra-ra !

THE POOR MAN.

I AM a very poor, poor man,
Alone I take my way;
I wish I could but once again
Be very glad and gay.

At home, in my dear parent's house,
A merry child was I;
Now want and sorrow are my lot,
Since in their grave they lie.

I see the rich man's garden bloom,
By golden fields I go;
But mine is still the barren path,
That leads through toil and woe.

Yet 'tis a mournful joy to me,
To pause where men are gay;
And heartily, with right good will,
I wish them all good day.

O bounteous God, Thou hast not left
Me utterly alone;
A comfort sweet for all the world,
Comes pouring from Thy Throne.

For yet by every village street,
Thy holy house they rear;
The organ and the solemn hymn,
These are for ev'ry ear.

Thy sun and moon, and beauteous stars,
Shed their pure light on me;
And when the bell at even sounds,
I seem to speak with Thee.

LION AND FOX.

MASTER Fox came up to the Lion one day,
" Now listen, your highness, to what I've to say—
I've been so put out that I can't go away.

" Concerning your highness the ass speaks not well,
He says—what men praise in you, he cannot tell;
That as to your courage, he feels a grave doubt,
You've done nothing noble that he can find out;
That you eat up the poor, and seek motives for strife
And praise you or love you he can't, for his life."

For a moment or two the great Lion was still,
Then said :—" Master Fox, let him talk as he will,
It would not become me to notice his bray,
Or value at all what a donkey may say."

THE OLD APPLE TREE.

I'M fond of the good old apple tree,
A very good-natured friend is he,
For knock at his door whene'er you may
He's always something to give away.

112

Shake him in Winter, on all below
He'll send down a shower of feathery snow;
And when the Spring sun is shining bright,
He'll fling down blossoms pink and white.

And when the Summer comes so warm,
He shelters the little birds safe from harm,
And shake him in Autumn, he will not fail
To send you down apples thick as hail.

Therefore it cannot a wonder be
That we sing Hurrah for the Apple-tree!

THE EMPEROR WHO BECAME A CARPENTER.

Now, there was once an Emperor,
A great and mighty man;
And when he said, " Do this—do that,"
A thousand servants ran.

The Emp'ror said,—" One thing I lack,
A ship to sail the sea,
The master who can build me one,
I'll pay him gallantly."

The Emperor who became a Carpenter.

And forth to seek a shipwright good,
They sent to east and west;
But in the land there was not one
Could do his lord's behest.

The Emperor was angry then,
And laid aside his crown,
" Then I must work myself," he said,
And from his throne came down.

And left his land, and seized an axe,
And wrought for daily pay;
And thus became a carpenter
For many a weary day.

Till he could build a stately ship,
With mast, and flag, and vane;
And then he joyfully went home,
To take his crown again.

You children, who your daily task,
Too often wish to shirk,
Think of the man who built the ship,
The Emperor who could work !

THE LITTLE LAMB.

A LITTLE lambkin, white as snow,
　Went feeding with its brothers,
And raced and frolicked to and fro,
　More wildly than the others.

It ran and sprang o'er stick and stone,
　And no one could prevent it;

The Little Lamb.

"Stop!" cried the mother, "little one,
    Or surely you'll repent it."

The little lamb went racing still,
    And frolicked all the faster;
Till, by a neighbouring rocky hill,
    It met with dire disaster.

A great stone lay there on the grass,
    Our lamb must needs jump o'er it,
And fell, and broke its leg, alas!
    Now sorrow lay before it.

I've told this little tale, dear child,
    That thou this lesson learnest,
The sport that's careless, rude, and wild,
    May change to bitter earnest!

THE KIND HOST.

Oh, of a host right kind and good,
 I've been a guest ere now,
The sign of his house, in the gay green wood,
 Was an apple that swang from a bough.

It was the merry apple tree
 With whom I went to dwell,
With food and with drink as sweet as might be,
 He entertained me well.

A hundred other guests at least,
 To meet me came flying along,
They hopped and they fluttered, and held a feast
 And each of them knew a song.

On the fragrant moss so fresh and green,
 The softest of beds was made,
My host spread o'er me himself, I ween,
 His comforting genial shade.

And when I asked what I had to pay,
 He shook his head so high ;
Good luck to my gallant host alway,
 Root, branch, and crown, say I !

IN THE CORN FIELD.

We've ploughed our land, and with even hand
The seed o'er the field we've strown;
But sunshine and rain, to ripen the grain,
Can be given by God alone.

The seed that springs, and the bird that sings,
And the shining summer sun,
The tiny bee, and the mighty sea,
God made them, every one.

Then, thankful we'll be, for shall not He
Who gives to each bird a nest,—
To each bee a flower, for its little hour,
Give his children food and rest?

THE BIRD AND THE MAID.

There sat a bird on the elder-bush,
    One beauteous morn in May;
And a little girl 'neath the elder-bush,
    That beauteous morn in May;

The bird was still while the maiden sang,
And when she had done his song outrang;

The Bird and the Maid.

And thus in the rays of the bright spring sun,
The maid and the bird sang on and on—
That beauteous morn in May.

And what I pray, sang the bright bird there,
That beauteous morn in May ;
And what was the song of the maiden fair,
That beauteous morn in May ?

They were singing their thanks to God above,
For the bounteous gifts of his priceless love,—
O ! such songs of praise,
Should be sung always,
Each beauteous morn in May !

————   · ·

As many stars as on winter nights
Shine out from the sky's deep blue ;
As many lambs as on summer days
Are sporting the meadow through ;
As many birds as in sweet spring-time
Fly forth o'er the sunlit lea ;
So many kisses I'd like to send,
Dear mother mine, to thee.

CHRISTMAS TREE.

Hurrah! we've got him—the Christmas-tree,
That all the children love to see,
He stood forlorn in the copse below,
And his outstretched arms they were stiff with snow.

A Merry Story.

I should like to know what presents bright
Will hang on his branches to-morrow night;
But, hush! we won't ask any questions yet;
To-morrow will show what each will get.

Hurrah! the fields are all white with snow,
But green as ever his branches glow;
In winter or summer no change knows he,
He's always our dear old Christmas-tree!

A MERRY STORY.

The dumb man said to the blind man:
" The harper I want to-day,
So tell me, have you seen him,
When he passed by this way?
Not that I care for harping
Myself, as it might appear,
But I wish he'd play me something
For my deaf son to hear."

The blind man said, " This moment
I've seen the very one,
And here's my leg-less servant,
To bring him he shall run;"

A Merry Story.

The leg-less man, obedient,
Went tramping up and down,
And ran, to find the harper,
Through all the streets in town.

Right quickly came the harper
His honoured friends to meet,
He had no hands, the harper,
He played with both his feet;
He played, until, to hear him
The deaf man was all aglow,
The blind man stared with wonder,
And the dumb man cried "bra-vo!"

The leg-less man fell a dancing,
And sprang with main and might,
The company kept together
Till day gave place to night.
And when at last they parted,
Right pleased was every one;
And so I hope will you be,
For all this is only fun.

" FOR WANT OF A NAIL."

THE master rode, 'twas for him to ride,
While his faithful servant ran by his side;
My lord rode on over stock and stone,
The other wearily tramping on.

" *For Want of a Nail.*"

Yet by his master's side kept he,
The faithful servant, and fears to see
Him fall so heavily.

"My lord, my lord," doth the servant shout,
A nail from your horse's shoe fell out,
And if the nail be not fastened on
Your horse's shoe will be lost and gone."
" Then let the nail go, friend ; what care I ?
The shoe hath more nails to hold it by,
And keeps on readily."

Again is heard the warning tone—
" My lord, from the hoof the shoe is gone ;
And unless you fasten it quickly on,
Your horse I fear will be lost and gone."
" Let the shoe go, friend ; what care I ?
The horse hath more shoes, and he may try
To keep on steadily."

And ere the servant again can cry,
He hath struck on a stone that lay close by ;
Down falls the steed and can rise no more,
And the master's reign of pride is o'er ;
He cries no longer now " What care I ?"—
He rises slowly, and marches by
With his servant, wearily.

THE CHICKENS AND THE HAWK.

Forth from the barn, the hen
Led chickens eight, nine, ten—
Through the yard the little rout
Ran so gaily round about,
Scratching in the yellow ground,
Gleeful when a prize they found.

125

The Chickens and the Hawk.

" At once," cried out the hen,
" Come chickens, eight, nine, ten!
Run to shelter, for I spy
Yonder hawk that wheels on high."
Quickly ran those chickens there—
Upward gazing in the air.

Right saucily, cried then,
Those chickens eight, nine, ten—
" Does our mother mean, I wonder
That small speck that's floating yonder,
And she raises such a cry
For that little beetle-fly?"

But down the hawk swooped then
Upon those chickens ten—
And the little saucy crowd,
Saw their danger, screamed aloud.
And the mother, with dismay,
Saw the hawk bear two away.

INDUSTRY.

GATHER roses while they bloom,
  Never lose a day,
Nor in sloth one hour consume,—
  Time doth pass away.

Now you've opportunity
  Both for work and play;
Where may you to-morrow be?—
  Time doth pass away.

Men have mourned their whole life through
  One good deed's delay;
Do at once what you've to do,—
  Time doth pass away.

CRADLE SONG.

SLEEP, baby, sleep,
Thy father keeps the sheep,
Thy mother shakes the little tree,
Then falleth down a dream for thee.
    Sleep, baby, sleep.

Sleep, baby, sleep,
The sky is full of sheep,

127

The lambs are little stars of light,
The shepherd is the moon so bright.
    Sleep, baby, sleep.

Sleep, baby, sleep,
And I'll give thee a sheep,

The Chapel.

All with a chain of gold so fine,
And it shall be the playmate thine.
Sleep, baby, sleep.

THE CHAPEL.

On the hill-side stands the chapel,
  Looking on the valley deep,
Where, by stream and valley singing,
  Blithe the herd-boy tends his sheep.

Hark! the little bell tolls sadly!
  See the mourners mount the hill;
And the boy's glad voice is silent,
  And he listens grave and still.

Yonder to the grave are carried
  Those who here were blithe and gay;
Little herd-boy, little herd-boy,
  Thus they'll toll for thee one day.

THE FOUR SEASONS.

Birds are in the woodland, buds are on the tree,
Merry Spring is coming, ope the pane and see.

Then come sportive breezes, fields with flow'rs are gay,
In the woods we're singing, through the Summer day.

The Daisy.

Fruits are ripe in Autumn, leaves are sere and red,
Then we glean the corn-field, thanking God for bread.

Then at last comes Winter, fields are cold and lorn,
But there's happy Christmas, when our Lord was born.

Thus as years roll onward, merrily we sing,
Thankful for the blessings all the seasons bring.

THE DAISY.

Now say, what has the daisy done
That no one hath a song begun,
Wherein is modestly set forth
The pretty simple flow'ret's worth?
I'll of the daisy sing to-day,
And in its praise shall be my lay.

The worth of things, we often find,
Is wrongly judged by human mind;
At some things, " Wonder !" still we cry ;
In others, beauty 'scapes our eye ;
And seeing nought we onward pass—
And this is just the daisy's case.

The Daisy.

In proper time the daisies may
Rejoice our hearts like roses gay ;
Who values not the daisy ne'er
Shall sit among our circle here :
For we will sing a daisy-song—
Who likes it not may hold his tongue.

Full well you all, dear children, know,
How February's clothed in snow ;
Let once the thaw-wind sweep the plain,
And lo ! the daisy blooms again,
'Mid winter's raging strife to be
A token of Spring's victory.

And when that herald I espy
I feel my heart is bounding high—
It seems as though in joyful guise
To life renew'd all dead things rise ;
And Death says to me, with a smile,
" My subjects sleep but for a while !"

In Autumn, too, I often see,
When wither'd leaves drop off the tree,

The Two Travellers.

The daisy blooms in beauty on
As if its morn were not yet gone ;
Heaven grant that once my autumn hour
May be like that of daisy-flower.

I pity much the foolish wight
Who holds the daisy's value light ;
Who little beauties can despise,
On greater things will close his eyes ;
And thus to teach us all thy worth,
Thou little modest flower, stand forth !

THE TWO TRAVELLERS.

THERE went two travellers forth one day,
To a beautiful mountain they took their way ;
The one,—an idle hour to employ,
The other to see,—to learn,—to enjoy.

And when from their journeying homeward they came,
There crowded around them master and dame ;
And a storm of questions from great and small—
" Now, what have you seen ?—Pray tell us all !"

The Two Travellers.

The first one yawned as he answer made,
" Seen ?—Why little enough !"—he said—

" Trees and meadows, and brook, and grove—
And song-birds around, and sunshine above."

Morning Song.

The other gave smiling the same reply—
But with brightening face and flashing eye,
" Oh, trees and meadows, and brook and grove,
And song-birds around, and sunshine above."

MORNING SONG.

Now the dark night hath passed away,
Now sings the lark, now dawns the day,
And see, the bright sun, from on high,
Shines down upon us wondrously.

It shines upon the monarch's hall,
It shines upon the beggar's stall,
And what lay hid in darkest night
It brings full clearly to the light.

Then let us thank and praise the Lord,
Who to us shelter deigned afford,
And with His holy angels kept
His helpless children while they slept.

Morning Song.

For many closed their eyes in pain,
And never saw the light again;

Then thank and praise Him, every one,
On whom shines down the blessed sun.

136

A CHILD'S CHRISTMAS CAROL.

(Sung three hundred years ago.)

From heaven high I've wander'd forth,
To bring glad tidings down on earth ;
Good store of tidings glad I bring,
Whereof I'll speak, whereof I'll sing.

For unto you a child this morn
Is of a chosen Virgin born ;
A beauteous Child, so fair to see,
Your joy and comfort it shall be.

For he is Jesus Christ our Lord,
Who unto all shall help afford ;
To be our Saviour He doth deign
To cleanse us from each sinful stain.

Salvation 'mong you He will share
That God the Father did prepare,
That in the heavenly kingdom ye
Might come to dwell eternally.

Chriſtmas Carol for Children.

Then mark ye well the signs He chose,
The lowly crib, the swaddling clothes;
There lieth, as an infant small,
He whose great power sustaineth all.

Let us rejoice, then, ev'ry one,
And with the shepherds wander on,
To see the gift the God of Heaven
For us in His dear Son hath given.

Awake my soul, and lift thine eyes,
Behold what in yon manger lies!
Who is this beauteous babe so mild?
It is the lovely Jesus-Child.

All hail to Thee! Thou heavenly guest,
Who scorn'st not us, by sin opprest,
But helpest all our misery—
How shall we thank Thee worthily?

O Thou that didst all things create,
How hast Thou ta'en such lowly state,

Chriſtmas Carol for Children.

To make the wither'd grass Thy bed,
On which the kine and oxen fed!

And if one mass were all this earth
Of gold, and gems of priceless worth,
Too small and mean it still would be
To form a cradle, Lord, for Thee.

No silks and velvets here are Thine,
Coarse swaddling clothes Thy limbs entwine,
Mid these, Thou King so rich and great
Dost shine, as in Thy heavenly state.

O Jesus! whom my soul holds dear,
Make unto Thee a cradle here;
Deign Thou to dwell within my heart,
That I may ne'er from Thee depart.

Then blest I evermore shall be;
Then shall I ever sing of Thee;
My grateful carols oft shall rise
In songs rejoicing to the skies.

A Cradle Elegy.

Glory to God upon the throne,
Who sendeth us His blessed Son !
Such strains the angel hosts employ,
To sing this new year's bliss and joy !

A CRADLE ELEGY.

Baby, sleep on mother's arm,
Safe from danger, safe from harm,
Buzzing flies shall not annoy,
Mother's love shall guard her boy.

One doth watch for thee and me,
Child and mother guardeth He;
Men and children, great and small,
Sleep in His protection all.

Baby, sleep on mother's arm,
Safe from danger, safe from harm,
Buzzing flies shall not annoy,
Mother's love shall guard her boy.

THE KING'S BRAVE SON.

THE old grey-headed king he sits
    Upon his father's throne ;
His mantle gleams like the evening red,
    Like the sinking sun his crown.

"Come ye, my first and my second son,
    I'll give to you my land ;

141

But thou, my third, my fav'rite son,
    What seek'st thou at my hand?"

" Of all thy treasures give me none
    But the old and rusted crown,
And three good ships, and I will go
    And find for myself a throne."

A SONG OF THE SEA.

THE sea is deep and the sea is broad;
But the glorious power and might of God
Is deeper far than the sea's deep ground,
Is wider far than the earth's wide round.

And many fishes swim to and fro,
And the Lord looks kindly on all below,
And leads them wondrously up and down,
And giveth his meat to every one.

And high as the raging waves may go,
At His command are they all laid low;
And thus He leads with His faithful hand
The ship all safe to the farthest land.

THE RICHEST PRINCE.

ONCE, as many German princes
    Feasting sat at knightly board,
Each began to boast the treasures
    He within his lands had stored.

Cried the Saxon—" Great and mighty
    Is the wealth, the power I wield,
For within my Saxon mountains
    Sparkling silver lies conceal'd."

" Mine's the land that glows with beauty !"
    Cried the ruler of the Rhine ;
" In the valleys yellow corn-fields,
    On the mountains noble wine !"

" Wealthy cities ! spacious castles !"
    Lewis said, Bavaria's lord ;
" Make my land to yield me treasures
    Great as those your fields afford."

Wurtemberg's belovèd ruler,
    Everard, called " the Bearded," cries,
" I can boast no splendid cities ;
    In my hills no silver lies ;

" But I still can boast one jewel,
  Through my forests, wandering on,
All my subjects know me—love me—
  I am safe with every one."

Then the princes, all together,
  Rose within that lofty hall;
" Bearded Count, thou'rt rich," they shouted,
  " Thou art wealthiest of us all!"

THE WATCHMAN'S SONG.

LISTEN, townsmen, hear me tell
Ten hath struck upon our bell;
God hath given commandments ten
That we might be happy men.
      Nought avails that men should ward us,
      God will watch and God will guard us.
      May He, of His boundless might,
      Give unto us all good night.

TO THE LARK.

IN the sun's bright gold,
O'er mountain and wold,
  Thy gladsome song doth ring :
As thou fliest free
Through the azure sea,
  Cooling thy airy wing.

The Bible.

Where the light cloud soars,
Where the torrent pours,
   Canst thou flit o'er the mountain's brow ;
Then down at a bound
From the sky to the ground—
   Oh, a glorious life hast thou !

THE BIBLE.

The Bible is a holy book,
   It tells of God and Heaven,
And teaches us to Heaven to look,
   Whence all good things are given.

Dear mother, teach me soon to read
   This holy book, I pray ;
Then God will help us in our need,
   And bless us day by day.

TAILLEFER THE BRAVE.

(A Rhyme of Hastings Fight.)

It was the Norman William who loudly did call—
" Who singeth in my court-yard? Who sings in my hall?
Who singeth at even? Who sings all day long,
And makes my heart to leap at the sound of his song?

" It is my bondman Taillefer who ever doth sing,
Standing in the court-yard, the draw-wheel to swing;
In hall whene'er the wood-fire he kindles and rakes—
At even ere he slumbers, at morn when he wakes."

Then out spake Duke William—" A good serf is he,
For Taillefer he serveth me right faithfullie;
He serves me in the court-yard, he serves at the well,
His minstrelsie it maketh my bold heart to swell."

Then out spake good Taillefer—" And if I were free,
I'd do thee better service, and still sing for thee;
How merrily on horseback my sword I might wield—
How would I sing and serve thee with sword and with
    shield."

Taillefer the Brave.

Nor long the time ere Taillefer rode forth to the field,
All on a gallant war-steed, with sword and with shield;
Look'd on him from the tower the Duke's sister fair—
"Perdie," she cried, " a hero, I ween, rideth there."

And pricking past the turret where lean'd the fair form,
He sang, now like a zephyr and now like a storm;
" How blithely," cried the lady, " his song doth out-
    pour!
It shakes my heart within me—it shakes e'en this tower!"

Nor long the time e'er William would sail o'er the sea,
To England would he wend with a great companie;
He sprang from out the ship, and he fell on his hand;
" Ha!" cried he, " thus I seize thee, and hold thee,
    England!"

Now when the Norman army to battle-field strode,
Before the Norman Duke noble Taillefer rode;
" For many a year I've kindled the fire in thy hall—
For many a year I've wielded the sword at thy call;

" And if a trusty servant I've still sung for thee,
Been first thy faithful bondman and then thy vassal free,
Then be this day my guerdon, to deal to the foe,
When first we ride against him, the first gallant blow."

Taillefer the Brave.

In sight of all the army rode Taillefer a-field,
All on his gallant war-horse, with sword and with shield ;
His song like sound of trumpet o'er Hastings' field roll'd :
He sang the songs of Roland, and good knights of old.

And when the song of Roland went pealing afar,
The banners blew out proudly—the men long'd for war ;
Then burn'd each Norman bosom, impatient with ire,
And still sang bold Taillefer, and still stirr'd the fire.

Then bravely rode he forward to deal the first thrust,
And soon an English horseman lay biting the dust ;
And high he swung his falchion, and smote the first blow,
Thereby an English horseman was quickly laid low.

The Normans saw his valour, nor tarried they long,
With clashing shields rode forward, with war-cry and
  song—
And then the weapons clatter'd, and blush'd rosy red,
Till on the field lay Harold, and Saxon churls fled.

The Norman Duke at evening his banner spread forth,
And pitch'd his tent where thousands lay dead on the
  earth,
And there he sat carousing with wine cup in hand,
And on his head the gold crown of merry England.

149

" Stand forth, my noble Taillefer ! Come, drink to me,
 ho !
Thy song hath ofttime pleased me, in weal and in woe ;
But on the field of Hastings thy clash and thy cry
Shall echo in my ear till the day that I die !"

THE BEE.

THERE was a little busy bee,
Cheerfully to and fro flew she,
Drawing and drawing continually
 Sweets from every flower.

Then the gardener's daughter came out,
And saw the little bee roving about,
And said, " In some flowers there's poison,
  no doubt,
 Yet on all, little bee, you hover."

" Certainly," answer'd the little bee,
" I meet with poison occasionally ;
But I find in each something good, you see,
 And I meddle not with the poison."

RETRIBUTION.

THE henchman his gallant lord hath slain,
The henchman to be a lord is fain.

He hath stabbed him dead, in the deep, dark wood,
And hath sunk the corpse in the deepest flood.

The Camel.

His master's armour the wretch doth don,
And mounteth his master's steed upon.

But when o'er the river bridge he'd ride,
The stolen horse rears, and swerves aside ;

When he strikes the golden spurs in its side,
It flings him into the foaming tide,—

With hand and with foot doth he struggle and row,
But the stolen armour drags him below.

THE CAMEL.

To the tune of a fife with its piercing tone
   And a big drum's hollow sound,
A stately camel came marching on,
   All Lisbon's city round.

The doors and windows threw open wide
   When they heard his footsteps fall,
And a thousand critics, " O wonder !" cried,
   In praise unanimous all.

Then cried a courtier, " Look there, look there,
   How nobly it bows the knee ;"

The Camel.

"And see," said a prince, "it will burdens bear
And carry, and silent be."

"How high it carries its lofty head,
  And its neck curved like a swan,"
A haughty vain young damsel said—
  And she proudly toss'd her own—

"Silence, pert thing!" her grandame says
  (For she was a well-known scold),
"Let me tell you 'twill fast for days and days,
  Like the monks austere of old."

And then a crook-back'd man came by,—
  "The best of all," said he,
"Is the hump it bears on its back so high,
  At least so it seems to me."

Such is the judgment of men! they praise
  What doth with themselves agree;
They like the man who reflects their ways,
  If even their faults have he.

COMING OF SPRING.

Open your windows and open your hearts !
Spring-time is coming and winter departs !
Old Winter he wishes to be let out,
And all through the house goes tripping about ;
His old grey cloak to his breast he strains,
And he's scraping together his frozen gains.

Open your windows and open your hearts !
Spring-time is coming and winter departs !
Here at the town-gate Spring is near,
So give poor old Winter a tug by the ear,
And pluck his old beard of hoary grey,
For that's the merry young fellow's way.

Open your windows and open your hearts !
Spring-time is coming, and winter departs !
The Spring is here, and he will come in,
He comes with music and merry din ;
He's rapping and tapping with main and might,
And ringing with flower-bells blue and white.

154

THE BOY AND THE ASS.

" Donkey, I'll ask you a riddle to-day—
What is that creature whose hide is gray,
Whose ears are large, and whose sense is small,
Who cries ' Ye-aw !' and walks with a lazy crawl?"
" Dear boy, that's too hard and too deep for me,
Pray tell me what may this creature be?"

Then the boy laugh'd loudly, and said, " Go to,
You foolish donkey, I spoke of you."
The ass prick'd his ears, but could not make out
Whatever the boy was talking about.
And the child went away—he was wrong, I confess,
For who'd give a donkey a riddle to guess?

THE GLOW-WORM.

SEE yonder glow-worm, the tiny thing,
That gleameth as if it were a king;
Whose breast like a little star doth blaze,
As from flower to flower in the grass it strays,
  So joyous, blithe, and free.

The Lioness and her Cubs.

How great must He be, how good, who could form
With such perfect wisdom that tiny worm !
Who decked it out in its shining dress,
And filled its small life with happiness,—
The God whom we cannot see.

THE LIONESS AND HER CUBS.

(From the German of Hans Sachs, the Cobbler-poet)

He who on others brings distress
Sows for himself unhappiness,
As happened to the lioness.

A lioness had made her den
For her two cubs in woodland glen ;
But once, while she was out for prey,
A hunter chanced to come that way.
He, ent'ring, found the cubs within,
And slew them both, and took the skin,
And onward went he through the wood.
Soon came the mother home with food,
And when she found her cubs were slain
She roar'd in mingled rage and pain,
And wept and grieved full bitterly.
That heard an old fox passing by,
And said, " Good sister, why this wail ?"

The Lioness and her Cubs.

The lioness her woes did tell,
With plenteous tears and groans and cries.
Then spake the fox, in cunning wise :—
"To know thy age full fain am I."
Whereto the lioness made reply :—
"Almost a hundred years I own."
"Now tell me true," the fox went on,
What all this time hath been thy meat,
Since thou hast dwelt in this retreat ?"
"My meat," the lioness did own,
"Hath been the flesh of beasts alone—
As hares and foxes, hart and hind,
And what I in the wood might find."
The fox said—"And were these thy food ?
Had they not fathers and mothers good ?
Then thou this self-same wrong hast done,
For ev'ry creature loves its young
As much as thou hast loved these twain.
How often hast thou given pain,
When thou their little cubs didst eat ?
Now with that measure thou didst mete,
It measured is again to thee,
Thou may'st believe me certainly."

> They who to others bring distress
> Make for themselves unhappiness,
> Remember this, sad lioness !

158

THE LION AND THE WOLF.

THE lordly lion and worshipful bear
  Sat once on the judgment-seat ;
And every beast, from largest to least,
  Stood marshal'd in order meet.

Then forth came sadly a good old cow,
  And said in sorrowful plight—
" Some rascally thief, to my infinite grief,
  Has stolen my calf, last night."

King lion look'd round the circle of beasts,
  To see who had aught to say ;

The Lion and the Wolf.

Cried the wolf, " I declare, and solemnly swear,
   This happen'd when I was away."

" And pray who accused you?" the lion said ;
   " Sir king, it's out of the question ;
It can't have been I, and I'll tell you why,—
   I suffer from indigestion."

" Be silent, robber !" the king cried out,
   " Your conscience is speaking true ;
Your's is the crime, and without loss of time,
   The bear shall do justice on you."

So the wolf was slain, and the story says
   He spoke his own condemnation ;
He's a guilty elf, who defends himself,
   Against nobody's accusation.

www.ingramcontent.com/pod-product-compliance
Lightning Source LLC
Chambersburg PA
CBHW030901050726
47500CB00009B/773